FORBIDDEN FUTURES PRESENTS

# MAXUS

written by

**Matthew M. Bartlett**

artwork by

**Mike Dubisch**

FORBIDDEN FUTURES PRESENTS #2 Published by ODDNESS.  ISBN: 978-1-7322124-6-6  Printed in the USA.

FORBIDDEN FUTURES PRESENTS

# MAXUS

written by

**Matthew M. Bartlett**

artwork by

**Mike Dubisch**

The warrior fell to his knees in the sand, overtaken by exhaustion from his frantic flight, and from bearing up against the cold. The columns of the ruined amphitheater—his intended destination—stood impossibly far off; against the backdrop of the black cliffs, they resembled nothing more than a thatch of bleached twigs. The sand held the cold of the two ice-suns in its endless sweep; it burnt his battle-scarred knees like the points of a million needles. He was almost beyond caring. In fact, he thought, it might not be the worst thing to fall forward, face down, let the cold subsume him until he was safe from all pain. Let it scar his eyes. Let it fill his mouth and ears. Let it pull him into the earth and add his sad senryu to the great comminuted anthology of dust.

*A sudden rhythmic percussion of explosions from the west pulled him from this miasmic malaise, brought him to his feet. He turned his head toward the sound. A figure in a cloak and five-pointed hood crested the horizon, a penumbra of disturbed air shimmering around it; beyond it, in the far distance, clouds of sand billowed skyward with each explosive burst.*

*That. That would be worse than dying here in this desert.*

For the warrior, who was called Maxus, knew all too well the provenance of the hood and the thing that wore it, the deathless psychic agony it could bestow. It would be worse than the certain torture and death that lay whence he came.

After a moment of indecision, he decided to take his chances moving forward, trying to evade the figure or, at worst, try to close his tired mind to its deadly whispered maledictions. With newly discovered strength, he angled his path away from it, but it changed its own trajectory. Panic took his heart, for whatever evasions he attempted, the other headed directly for him. And when they met, when the two were less than a yard apart, he saw that the hood framed no face, but rather a shifting sequence of colors: a moment of glinting yellow, one of gunmetal grey, and one char-black, all followed by the briefest flash of red, the shifts matching the continued beat of the blasts. With each transition from color to color the scenery behind the figure twitched and flickered like old film in a dilapidated projector. And somehow, there through the entirety of the sequence, a glinting, eternal blackness, the depth of which hollowed out his stomach. "I am not your enemy, but rather your Benefactor," a slithering voice said. "You must write one last piece, and then I will reveal my true face."

And the cliffs buckled and the columns went to powder and the colors leached from the hood and seared Maxus's face, and there sounded a chorus of screams as his eyelashes caught light, and he woke to an ebbing echo of sobbing laughter as real as the workaday traffic outside.

Reginald Rose, under the name Maxus R. Crowther, once wrote of otherworldly realms where phantasmic magic clashed with fire-swaddled bludgeons in fields of stone; of fire-lit marshes where seekers of proscribed knowledge clashed with hordes of the miry dead; of taciturn warriors and learned, loquacious clerics. His imagination had seemed to him an endless well, his muse generous and fertile. Now, in the double-fisted grip of arthritis and old age, he could not without great effort depress the keys of a typewriter long enough to write a simple sentence. In fact, he could scarcely scribble his once glorious, ornate signature on the rent check, whose four-digit sum was a laughable misrepresentation of what he could afford to pay for the coming month's rent.

He'd started writing before he'd reached his teens, inspired by a book of Fantasy art that a middle school classmate had smuggled into the cafeteria. His friends had gathered around, gawking at the bosomy warrior women in revealing animal-skin skirts and elegant princesses with long, bare legs and cocked eyebrows. Reginald was not unmoved, but what truly captured him were the elaborately rendered landscapes and cityscapes, populated with hard-bitten warriors, hooded warlocks, and impossible beasts, rendered by artists with wonderfully evocative names: Corbin San Bruno, B. Zelton D'Walter, Eammon Yop. Later, in the school library, he was able to find some of the books for which they'd done the covers, and he devoured them.

His own initial efforts consisted mainly of short pieces in ball-point pen in school examination books. A tale about a Warrior-Clown who commanded a squadron of Were-panthers. A vignette about a gory war between necromancers and ghouls. A fantasy in which a thin, sickly boy used ritual magic to command an army, and ultimately rule an empire.

His parents, his first readers, praised and encouraged him. They both were schoolteachers; his mother, a former folksinger who still performed at coffeehouses after work, taught mathematics. His father, a Middle School English teacher, had an appreciation for literature, but no interest in creating it. Reginald's schoolmates, however, hassled him mercilessly; gym class was a nightmare, and he spent recess in the school library.

"Where be Maxus?"

"We have but an odd number, and we need him."

"The bastard ruins everything."

The fisticuffers waited on the broad stone steps of the coliseum, some of them stretching, some flexing, some punching another's open palms, some desultorily chipping away at the concrete with their pocketknives. "You know where he is," said Phinehas.

"The library?"

"The library."

"Let him throw a book at a charging hexigorgoth."

"Or climb a musical scale to escape a horde of cothclarks."

"Who goes to get him today?"

"Lukachok."

"Oh, now, why me?"

"For your trouble, we'll pair you with him. And if you want to break a rule or two, we'll look the other way."

Lukachok took the library steps two at a time. All around him, books he would never open crowded shelves that towered into the dimness of the upper reaches. Clerics ascended and descended wheeled ladders, some retrieving books, some shelving books either returned by patrons or knocked from the shelves by one of the library's many cats. In the leaning shafts of sunlight, winged crabs wheeled, pests that would, if unchecked by the cats, lick the words from the books' very pages with their raspy tongues. Lukachok disliked the crabs. He disliked the cats. And he disliked the library, its musty reek, its dark corners untouched by natural light, its endless rows of books. Who had that much to say about anything?

He found Maxus sitting cross-legged in a corner, an annoyingly large book stretched across his lap, held up by his skinny knees. Maxus ran his finger along under each sentence, his lips moving. "You're wanted at fisticuffs," Lukachok said. "We need an even number of fighters."

"I'm done with fisticuffs," Maxus said.

"Don't like violence?"

Maxus smiled. "I love violence. I don't like it when it's not for keeps. And I don't like having to touch the likes of you."

*Lukachok's smile fled. He sneered, and with all his might he kicked the spine of the book. It flew upward, hitting Maxus in the face. Maxus stood, letting the book fall open to the floor. His eyes rolled back, showing only white, shot through with a web of red veins. The veins trembled. Maxus recited a four-word incantation. He repeated it. Lukachock trembled. He twitched.*

*And he blinked out of the library, leaving the searing odor of sweat and sulfur.*

*Maxus looked down. Lukachok now lived in the book. He'd been plunked down in the middle of a village with thatched huts and torches that burnt purple below a mucous-yellow sky.*

*He laughed when he saw the first sentence in which the pesky fisticuffer appeared.*

*"The intruder screamed and screamed as inside the huts, great beasts stirred and extended long, curved claws."*

*Let Lukachok take his chances with the monsters that roamed within.*

*A cat turned the corner, regarded Maxus, then set to grooming the back of its paw. "Now," Maxus told the cat. "The fisticuffers shall have an even number for their sport."*

**MAXUS by Matthew M. Bartlett**

High school and college saw Reginald's authorial ardor fade in favor of more practical pursuits. He fell in with the theater students, performed in plays and musicals, pursued girls, and even found time to study enough to attain passing grades. In college, he wrote almost nothing save the papers assigned to him, but he consumed with rapacity the poetry and classical literature to which his professors exposed him.

Upon graduating, he was right back to it, writing before and after work, filling reams of typing paper with more ambitious and wide-ranging tales. He researched the market and mailed out many manuscripts, at first with no success at all. When he got his first acceptance, he thought his heart might burst. More followed, and the thrill did not fade. The money was decent, but he received the checks with surprise, as though they were an unexpected bonus.

For years, despite his successes, Crowther remained an unknown. Some of his stories populated stapled and photocopied booklets in smudged typefaces. Others resided in the kind of magazines whose covers were hidden behind opaque barriers on the top shelves of newsagents. Therein, laid out in typo-ridden columns, his work sat ignored alongside garish photographs of hollow-eyed strumpets clad only in tall, shining boots and studded caps; pale waifs wielding braided whips; waifs succumbing with affected distress to the demands of waxed-mustache men clad in unconvincing surgical costumery. But most of his fiction remained unpublished, and lay in disordered piles of pages on every available horizontal surface in his tiny apartment.

One day he spotted in the local alternative newsweekly an advertisement for an annual Fantasy and Science Fiction writers' convention that happened to be scheduled on a weekend that coming summer, and within an hour's drive. He secured a ticket. The convention was a crowded, lively affair held in the meeting rooms and ballrooms and cafes of two upscale hotels that sat on either side of a small park of meandering, bench-lined footpaths; fountains; copses of trees; and duck-filled ponds.

He was awed to see in person some of the giants of the genre, Hisrick von Breezemouse and Vance Treadheck and Caleb Spraque and the like, roaming the halls like they owned them, with their sweeping coiffures and their ax-shaped sideburns, their wide lapels and wider ties, their monk strap shoes and their glasses full of iced amber liquids, the ever-present cigarettes, like extra limbs jutting from between elegant, intimidating fingers. Reginald slunk among them, too shy to approach, intimidated by their

erudite, lettered colloquies and insular kaffeeklatsches. At panel discussions of fantasy-related minutiae, themes, and concepts, he'd sat on a folding chair, scribbling notes, just another member of the audience, as the important writers sat behind brass nameplates at curtained tables, pontificating grandly on all matter of topics with an air of not-to-be-contradicted authority.

On the first morning, walking from the hotel to a gallery that was hosting a convention-adjacent exhibition, he fell into step with Gabriel Capricos, author of the famed Kyrg series, which had been optioned for television, and whose latest installment's release was being celebrated as one of the convention's premier events. Kyrg was a warrior-thief who stole magic-imbued eggs from the nests of giant, talking birds. He was built like a bodybuilder, wore elaborate armor, spoke little. By contrast, his creator Capricos was a bespectacled, bearded, acne-scarred fellow who carried his prodigious gut not like a burden, but like a bludgeon. He was clad in a brown tweed suit, his neck swaddled in a psychedelic ascot. His long, reddish-blond hair curled up at the ends, and his flecked, crusted lips struggled to cover a jumble of yellow teeth. The handle of his walking stick was a likeness of the author himself, albeit a younger, idealized rendition, with a shorter, neater coiffure, presumably commissioned at astronomical cost. Reginald was less than intimidated. After some general small talk, he said, "Do you have any advice for an author just starting out?"

Capricos stopped mid-step and turned with a dramatic flair, laying a beefy hand on Reginald's shoulder. "I have advice, but not for mere *authors*," he said, his voice breaking into a quasi-British accent, "but for *fantasists*. That, boy, is that, uh, which…that to which you should aspire."

"To be a…"

"A fantasist. Indulge me a moment. Picture yourself seated on a well-appointed cathedra. You're clad in a robe, your head adorned with a wingéd and hornéd helmet. You have the musculature of a warrior and the epigastrium of a lord. Across from you sits your muse, narrow of cheekbone, clad in a headpiece like the crown of the manta-bird, long gloves and elegant shoes, something sheer, one long, slender calf lain over the other. Ideas flow like smoke from her fingertips like smoke; words from yours. On the floor lays your cat—let's say he is become a great dragon. He provides the ineffable, the magic, straight from his soul and out through his flaring nostrils. These three streams merge and coalesce—they become something winged and fierce. Something separate. Independent. Beyond your ken and your control.

Without a muse, and without a familiar, son, you may yet reach your petty aspiration to be an author. With them, you have already reached that lofty title of fantasist."

And then, with characteristic gravity and portentousness, he abruptly ended the tête-à-tête and proclaimed he must locate a toilet forthwith, or else rue the day.

Reginald had one other close encounter with fame. On the afternoon of the last day of the three-day stretch, he'd ridden an elevator fifteen floors down with von Breezemouse, just the two of them, in a small box whose interior was dimmed mirrors, the serried accretion of reflections adding to the air of unreality, and hadn't mustered the courage to say anything. He'd scrunched himself into the corner, dizzied by the alcoholic fumes of the author's aftershave; his unexpected height, enhanced by the low elevator ceiling; the carrot-hued earwax staining his lobes; the amusing flatness of his buttocks, offset by the unnecessary broadness of his gaudy snakeskin belt. He'd later regretted dearly his inability to break the silence, when he read about the author's death a few years afterwards, of liver cancer, though he wondered if he'd might've regretted it more if he *had* said something. He could readily imagine hearing his own hasty, ill-chosen words echoing unpleasantly in his head forever after.

**MAXUS by Matthew M. Bartlett**

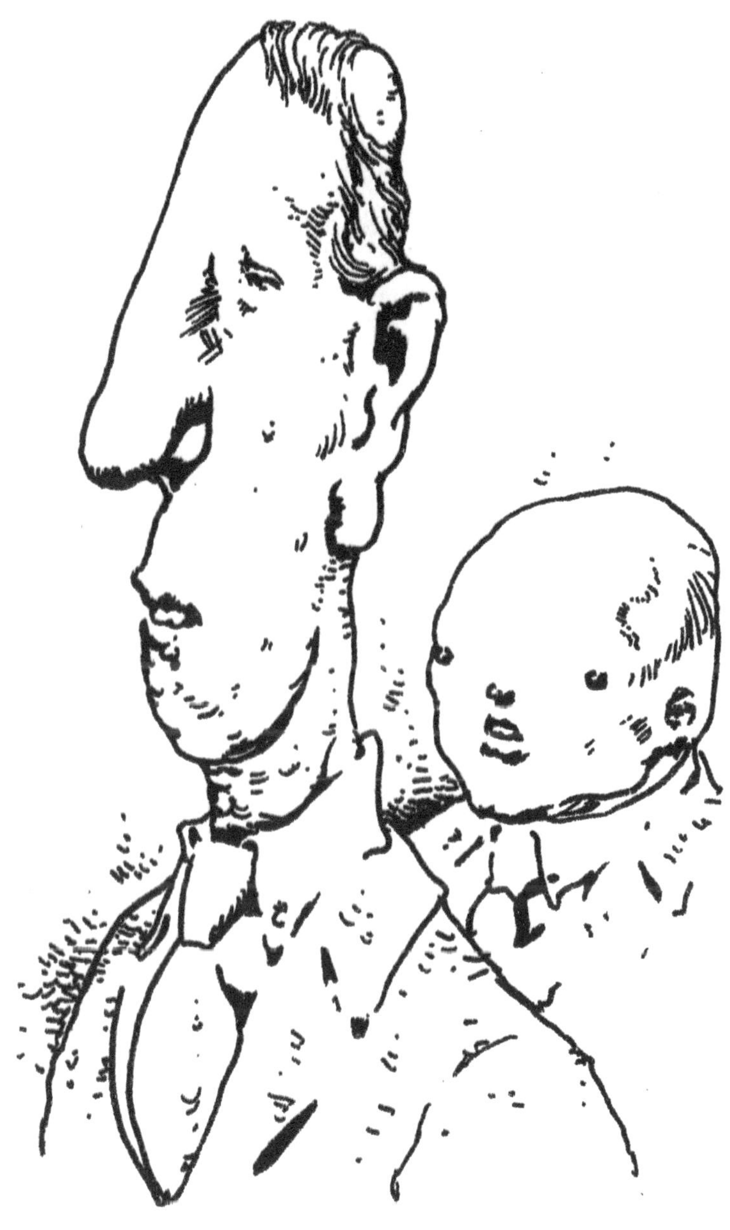

*Maxus slept. The curtains softly rustled, then swept into the room like great diaphanous wings. The song of the ferfets owned the night, drowning out the sound of the wind, the raucous singing from the taverns, the percussive noises from the inhabitants of the Vintic fields. As night reached its apex and rolled languidly downward, all noise but that of the ferferts faded. Then that faded too. The Farkahoryt River sent its colors of orange and periwinkle back up to the clouds, where they leached into the sky. The Kenker awoke, furious at the unwelcome return of consciousness, and unleashed its first affronted roar of the morning.*

*It was day.*

*In the* Vintic Fields *stood the dead giants, grey and stiff, where their wicked breed had met its end, via the combined forces of magicians who had pooled their powers to cast a collective spell that adhered their massive feet to the ground, bound their hands to their sides, and narrowed their throats so that their avian attendants may not find and feed them.* They'd *died, starved or stricken, where they'd made their last stand, in the rigid formation that spelled their defeat, everything above their knees covered in clouds, their decomposition hampered by a separate spell (the need for which the group was alerted to in a near panic by a hierophant).* Calcified *craters like massive barnacles peppered their calves. In these craters, in the legs of long-dead giants, in the* Vintic Fields, *men of lesser means made their homes.*

*In his, just above where the foot met the calf,* Maxus *rose.* He *gathered his hair and tied it back.* Hunger *gripped his gut.* As *he dressed, he heard a furtive noise below.* Across *from the bed, his battlehammers stood on their heads like sentries on either side of his chair, their handles ever anticipating his grip.* He *took them up, their weight at once a strain and a comfort. In the air, at his side, swinging at bodies, maiming and crushing—that was their good and right state, and he felt them flexing in anticipation of impact with flesh.*

Two *greasy grimfels scurried among the feet of the giants, dragging a sack of eyes.* The *eyes of the giants were more than just pretty; they were precious, fetching generous sums at the* Okkstoe Bazaar, *and they were considered the property of the men who lived in the* Vintic Fields. The *money they made from the sales was used to feed them, affect repairs, and the like.* The *eyes could not be manually excised from the sockets, due to the lingering effects of the magic that still held the dead giants in place. But three years previous, the first one had fallen on its own. Then, a month or so later, another. Now they fell from time to time, and were gathered by the Landlords of the Vintic Fields and held in their coffers until there were enough to bring to market. The coffers were supposed to be protected by guards.*

But grimfels were clever, and given to brutality. Maxus hoped they hadn't killed the guards. He leapt to the ground and lighted after the pair. He plunged through the river, past which the giants were thicker, closer together, facing outward from a central point at which had stood their leader, and then, past the border, giving way to the flora-canyons with their rough texture; their proliferation of trichomes, soft looking yet turgid; the cold, shadowed caves gouged into their surfaces, the rising sunlight limning their verdant parapets.

One of the grimfels rose up, its bony fingers gripping a spiked truncheon, the handle not much thicker than the creature that wielded it. It swung downward toward Marcus's head, but Maxus swung his hammer faster on a horizontal axis. It crashed into the grimfel's side, splitting the flesh, shattering the ribs to powder and shards, making a stew of the organs. The truncheon tumbled from the grimfel's hand as it fell heavily onto its side, curling up like a spider, wheezing high pitched shrieks from both its mouth and its profusely perforated lung. Its blood spurted into the air in fast, thick gluts.

The second grimfel snatched up the truncheon and whacked Maxus in the knee, then lighted for the hills. Maxus knelt, wincing. He rose for long enough to hurl his battlehammer.

*End over end it flew, its course unaltered by wind, its path not broken by any giant's leg. It caught the grimfel at the back of the neck, nearly decapitating it, and crushing the skull as it rotated. The grimfel staggered to its own knees, its distorted, knocked-askew features grimacing grotesquely at the uncaring sky. Maxus examined his knee with his fingers—the flesh was broken, but just, and he'd develop a hell of a bruise. The bones appeared to be intact, though the pain was enormous, exquisite. Wincing and cursing, he gathered the eyes that had fallen from the sack during the fracas, and limped toward home. He raised his eyes to see the guards, pulling blindfolds from their heads and gags from their mouths, walking towards him, gratitude shining in their eyes.*

After loading his suitcase into his car, Reginald wandered off in search of lunch, and eventually found himself in line at a sandwich cart. There he began a conversation with a small woman with big glasses and a brilliant, gap-toothed smile, a conversation interrupted only by the need to order and eat their food, the latter of which they did seated on a low stone wall outside a castle-like library. Her name was Gayle. She worked in the office of the hotel in which he was staying. She liked savory foods, crime novels, and funk. She was not the slender muse as envisaged by Gabriel Capricos, perhaps not a muse at all, but a sharp and funny human being, and she was the better for it. He would never forget the taste of that otherwise unremarkable Rueben.

The two courted for a time and then married. He felt it was a comfortable, homey marriage; he had no indication she felt otherwise. They congratulated themselves on their openness, their mutual respect. They lived comfortably on the combination of his proceeds from publication and her not insignificant salary, and were able to indulge in yearly vacations and frequent meals at restaurants.

Gradually, Reginald rose in prominence, his tales attaining places in the more heralded journals, magazines, and anthologies. Due to the efforts of his agent, several pieces were optioned for film adaptation; two were in development, one in turnaround. The big publishers circled. The couple had a house built in the country, designed by the renowned architect Willem Lyle Thatcher. Gayle confessed that she loved to tell her coworkers that her husband was a writer. She joined him at conventions when she could, or otherwise saw him off at the airport, cheered him on upon the publication of two novels and a collection, watched with barely contained joy as he found himself in the guest chairs of the late-night television hosts, where he was funny, charming, a curiously outsized version of the Reginald she knew.

It was five years into the marriage when Reginald flew in from Los Angeles and arrived home to find Gayle dead, an apparent suicide. She lay face-up in their marriage bed, nude, mouth full of foam. Scattered around her on the duvet were split capsules, yellow and red like condiment colors. An empty pint glass nestled at her side like a final companion. When he'd called her from LAX the night before, she'd sounded drowsy. They had a few friendly words. He couldn't remember exactly what they'd said. This was, in a way, a great relief, in another way it was torture.

There was no note. There had been nothing to indicate she had been unhappy. What had he missed? Thinking about it all made him feel desolate and frantic. So, once the service was complete, the body released to the custody of her distraught parents, the grim business of death conducted and concluded, he opted to not think about it. Sometimes he was successful. More so when he pulled his typewriter from under the bed and resumed writing. If in his work he touched upon the harrowing loss of Gayle, he was unaware of doing so. He certainly didn't try to.

The life insurance payout, a lump sum, helped him to settle up some longstanding debt on which he'd been paying installments, but was hardly sufficient to substitute for steady income. So he sold the house at a loss, rented a modest apartment, and cognizant of the vagaries of artistic revenue, took on full-time accounting work at a small firm.

He often wondered if by doing so, by not betting on his skill to keep him afloat, he was somehow responsible for the decline that followed. That was not, in fact, the case. Trends in Fantasy had changed; upcoming writers were signing multi-book and series deals, and their work (sent to him by publishers begging his endorsement) he found hopelessly effete: faery lands; fanciful monsters who were more pet than threat; pre-teen heroes in saccharine love stories cloaked in the gimcrack trappings of Fantasy. His contemporaries tucked away their own misgivings (he presumed) and dutifully followed suit. He could not. He found it all insufferable. And so Reginald Rose could only watch in helpless despair as his alter ego, Maxus R. Crowther, foundered and slid back downhill into relative obscurity. He still wrote, still sent manuscripts, to little avail. Eventually he stopped both. He found to his surprise that he did not miss it. What he had thought was a drive, an unstoppable push, an endless well, was just gone. Gone like Gayle. Gone like his youth.

He did not know of the small but fervent fandom that gathered in early online forums to discuss and celebrate his work. He would never know of them.

**That one time Maxus escaped the Battlehawk nest....**

*Winter. The wind was blades and spikes of ice, its shrieks and howls approximating frenzied speech: hysterical, furious, overlapping jeremiads of the panicked damned. Snow and ice crystals filled the air, scrambling every which way. For the first time since their cadaverous incarceration, the dead giants trembled, causing the ground beneath them to crack, fissures zig-zagging outward like terrestrial lightning. The cave-homes in the legs of the giants shook loose all that was not nailed down. Men perished, crushed under their own belongings, or swept out into the air only to plummet to icy ground, their splashed blood gluing their corpses down.*

*Maxus, whose residence was not far off the ground, crouched where he could watch the goings-on outside. In the frenzy of crystalline white, the snow formed patterns, perhaps words, or symbols impossibly complex, strung together in tantalizing semi-coherence. It was hypnotic, mesmerizing.*

And then it was over. All at once. The snow whisked itself away. The wind sank to whispers and then went silent. A glassy sun oozed out through the lingering haze as the clouds lifted. Somewhere, someone sobbed. Then rose cries of agony, cries of despair, cries for help.

Maxus looked about his room. Most of the glass still intact. A chair sat forlornly amongst its broken-off legs. Books lay scattered, some with bent pages. A great wave of relief swept over him when he saw that his dressing mirror, which had fallen onto its face, was intact. The mirror had been a gift, presented to him by the Elders of the distant city of Oclopolis, which he'd helped defend against a savage horde of reanimated Psuedo-Clorfs, which the Elders could not through magic dispel, their powers having been briefly disabled by a spell of impediment. The mirror rotated top to bottom or side to side, affixed a frame of ornate design. He had never used it, was un-

clear, in fact, as to the exact nature of its functionality and features. His benefactors had provided him with a hasty explanation, beyond what his interpreters could fathom, though the latter did put forth a valiant effort before shrugging in bemused defeat.

He stepped in front of it. He regarded himself, the lines of middle age on his face, bracketing his features, the still-proud chin under the wisp of greying beard, the eyes, whose youthful power was now dulled by battle and by grief. He had stood before the mirror previously, trying to engage its magic to no avail, but now something was different. A nearly palpable electricity in the air. His body tingled, first the extremities, then all of him. The sensation was nearly erotic, the light brushing of a thousand female fingertips on the outside of his dermis and, almost unbearably, on the inside as well.

The room shimmered behind him. His feet rose out of his slippers. His legs shortened and withered as his toes lengthened into talons, which spread themselves apart into great asterisks. He lifted his arms

*for balance, but they buckled and bent behind his back. He surrendered to the strange magic that was occurring, and his arms rose as wings behind him. His beard drew inward. His chin collapsed upward. His nose and mouth elongated into a snout of sorts, bent downwards at the end, and then hardened into a beak. His eyes wheeled wildly in his head. He opened his beak to exclaim—watched as his reflection did the same—and was shocked to hear a raspy squawk. His robe went black and became feathers.*

*Testing his new, slender legs, he walked on pointed toes to the balcony, and without hesitation, spread his wings, pushed up from the ground, and flew. Between and among the legs of the giants he sped, and then beyond them, the wind lifting his wings, his small heart thumping madly below his throat. Over the towers of the city he soared, the men below as small as blades of grass, surveying the damage of the storm. He glided over field and mountain, burg, town, city, and farm.*

*Far below, he espied the tattered tents and crushed caravans of the doomed Okkstoe Bazaar, the zig-zag line of the Farkahoryt, thicker now, having overrode its banks, disappearing into the valley between the* Oegnhorrt Mountains; *over pasture and plain; over the dead city of* Elayg-eten-Benure, *destroyed some time back by fire, its towers and tenements now subsumed by snow, save their charred upper edges, scrawled like hieroglyphics on the pure white surface.* He *saw the sweep of the great valley now, the two levels of fortifications that bracketed* Keirjl, *that treacherous city of domed rondavels, packed in tight like pox, each topped with a sentient gemstone, the walls but one byproduct of a lesson learned hard and at the cost of many lives, now just names scrawled like wistful poetry on those very bulwarks.* A *city of sluggards, scoundrels, and rogues, hostile to outsiders, best seen from afar.*

He *angled upward to the bottom of the clouds when he came to the warring cities of* Mabonatinn *and* Claqq, *each city housed in its own endlessly expanding superstructure, yet even at that lofty height, he still had to evade the columns of black smoke.* The *firing of the cannons below was as the muted percussion of staggering, stomping boots crushing bone.* He *dove down past the farther side of* Claqq, *to see if he could spy the armored* Queen, *who legendarily would not shy from battle.*

*And there she was, stalking the parapets, winding between the spiked palisades like an upright, winged spider. She wore shining black armor with retrofitted wings, each equipped with pockets for her bolts, head encased in a helmet with holes for her fierce horns, the whole ensemble a dark mirror that wrapped the surrounding landscape tightly around her body. She held her bow at her side, a war-knife at throat-level.*

*She spied him watching. She raised the spine of the knife to her brow, angled to block the sun's searing rays. Then something caught her eye below. A rogue regiment from Mabonatinn approached. She raised both arms and battlehawks launched themselves from the city's wells. They set upon the insurgents, stripping the flesh and muscle from their skeletons as easily as one might forcibly remove a coat from a child. The Queen cackled madly as her enemies' organs tumbled to the dirt and the battlehawks returned to their nests to share their prizes with their chicks.*

Now Reginald dwelt in the decrepit west end of the city, on an upper floor of a doddering tenement hemmed in by dirt courtyards behind sagging wire fences. The dull grey tower was identical to its many brethren, which lined an avenue bordering a river populated not with fish and frogs but with syringes and discarded prophylactics. Cracked windows shuddered in loose casements. Silverfish teemed in crevasses formed by split linoleum. Lights operated in defiance of the switches meant to ignite or extinguish them. Turning on the water resulted in thumping in the walls and the dribbling of discolored liquid. Patches of ceiling bulged, discolored and soft to the touch. Reginald saw it less as a tenement than hospice for the discarded, one bereft of carers. Often he fell asleep to the sound of the cries of people who, assuming they'd ever had control of their lives, had long since lost it.

Over the course of the last several months, those cries had been fewer and fewer. Some of the doors in the hallway he'd discovered open, looking in on apartments emptied of everything but crumbs, pennies, and cigarette butts. Occasionally someone would pound on his door, shouting, though he could not make out what they were saying. Maybe they were trying to drive him out with their incessant noise, the hollering and thumping, but he had absolutely no intention of leaving. He had an endless store of canned beans, meat, fish, and spinach, and he nibbled at them rarely and without pattern, washing them down with brown tap water.

The explosions started one day, out of nowhere. Sitting in his chair, watching the flickering image of some situation comedy on the television, he wondered if some war, some invasion, had begun. He scrawled the word WAR into the dust on the arm of his chair with an unclipped fingernail. He stood and looked out the window. The view was the same as always. No fighter jets strafing the city. No fires, no paratroopers dangling from helicopters, brandishing heavy machine guns. Just occasional grey smoke at the edges of the frame, smoke that dissipated quickly.

The next morning, the explosions sounded again, this time louder. Reginald's apartment shook and swayed. Finally, with much effort, he pushed himself up from his chair, The view from the west-facing windows was unchanged. He turned and walked to the door. When he opened it, light assailed him, bright and punishing. The apartment across from his was gone. Well, the floor was still there, bare concrete. But the wall between it and the hallway were gone, as was the wall to the outside. The wind pushed at his chest. Finally he was able to blink away the red spots that clouded his vision.

Angled across a bright, cloudless blue sky was the long, latticed boom of a crane, the sunlight glinting off the steel bars. Tethered to its tip by a long chain, something oblong swayed halfway to the ground. Then it got larger, larger still, gunmetal grey, a scuffed and paint-smeared industrial monstrosity. It crossed the sun's path, its edges glinting bright, blinding yellow. It filled his vision, char black. Then it retreated, blazing yellow, gunmetal grey, back to yellow, back to black, and again, and again, over and over, lulling Reginald into a dream state like the pendulum of a hypnotist's watch. Then, finally, it nearly disappeared in the distance, then flew in faster than it had thus far, filling the sky. The last thing he saw before it tore through the apartment floor and through him, dissolving all to powder, was a blackness darker than he'd ever dared imagine, even in fiction, and a flash of red.

## MAXUS by Matthew M. Bartlett

*Maxus had earned his repose. In his new home, granted to him by his admirers, in the forehead of the leader of the giants, central to the horde of the dead, he gazed down upon the surface of the clouds from his arched, cantilevered balcony. From time to time, attendants would lift him from his finely wrought golden chair so that he could tour his accumulated treasures: the set of shelves whose arch mirrored that of the balcony's aperture, the upper shelf home to a bronze oil lamp; the lower filled with well-maintained incunabula, grimoires, anti-bibles, and other tomes forbidden, rare, or otherwise precious, along with the skulls of the vanquished Mreo-Ad-Aschi and Fiunghrr the 8th; the low-slung table crowded with urns, phials, goblets, apothecary jugs, and flasks; its wide drawer that held broadsides, broadsheets, the notes and scribblings and sketches of long-gone magicians, that; the aperture afforded him views of the onion-domed towers of the nearby city. Attendants read to him, conveyed to him the news of the day, engaged him in rhetorical games and lively debate. They provided him an engaged and attentive audience when he felt the need to tell of his life's struggles, real, exaggerated, or entirely fabricated.*

*Often, the edges of his vision crinkled and wavered, blurred and faded. Songs and speeches he heard, but he knew not whether they were but phantasms of memory. He no longer knew whether he spoke to attendants or to an empty room. He could not recall his last nourishment, but he felt neither full nor hungry. He knew neither desire nor satisfaction, he knew not longing nor satiation. He knew not whether he was revenant or man. It did not matter, he supposed, on those rare and rarer occasions when there was a Maxus to suppose.*

MAXUS by Matthew M. Bartlett

**Matthew M. Bartlett lives in Western Massachusetts with his wife Katie Saulnier and an unknown number of cats. At present, he writes for his living.**

Graphic Novelist and Illustrator Mike Dubisch has been creating and publishing comics and art since the 1980's. Dubisch has carved out a unique place for himself in the world of art and comics, creating works of horror, science-fiction, surrealism, and YA adventure using all but lost traditional techniques. Born in California, USA, the artist has traveled the world and lived in five countries. Dubisch has been an instructor at the Academy of Art University since 2012, and is married to children's book illustrator and sculptor Carolyn Watson Dubisch with whom he has three daughters.

www.ingramcontent.com/pod-product-compliance
Lightning Source LLC
Chambersburg PA
CBHW030336310726
48979CB00001B/57
*9781960213020*